TAJ NIEVES

CONTENTS

CHAPTER 1
SANTA CLAUS IS COMING

The time was only a few strokes of the clock past midnight on Christmas morning. The night was freezing cold and snow fell from the heavens as tiny white specks. The ground was cold enough to sustain them. So, instead of quickly melting into tiny puddles of water, the snow collected into menacing white piles. The night was cold, severely cold.

The air was serene but eerily quiet, save for the chimes of the Christmas lights and other peculiar decorations that rang out Christmas jingles in the air. The streets were beautiful. Each house was decorated as best as the family could with lights and props.

The night was cold, but the heat was on. Which was why Anna found it strange that a chill had woken her up. Like a gust of cold air had blown in and washed over her.

She shivered and opened her eyes. She wondered where the wind was coming from and looked towards the large single window in the room.

It was wide open and the moonlight was streaming into the room.

Anna became confused because the window had not been open in days due to the cold wind that had been ravishing them.

"Mark, honey. Did you open the window? She asked nudging her sleeping husband lightly.

He didn't respond so she shook him even harder.

"Mark?" she asked confused and a little worried. His temperature had dropped and he wasn't even snoring like he usually did.

She rolled him from his side and saw that a portion of the bed was wet.

Frightened now, she quickly sat up and turned on the bedside lamp beside her.

The dull yellow glow from the lamp helped illuminate half of the room.

She looked at her husband under the light and was horrified. The wetness on the sheets had come from his neck and it was blood. His neck had been sliced open while he slept and the killer was nowhere to be found.

Anna screamed in fright.

"Mark." She cried as she shook him. His body wasn't cold yet so it meant it had happened recently. The killer was probably still in the house.

She curled her legs up to her chest as her eyes darted back and forth from the darker parts of the room, looking for who it was that had killed him.

"You better watch out… you better not cry. You better not pout… I´m telling you why." A voice sang menacingly from beneath her. "Santa Claus is coming to town." The voice sang on.

Anna jumped in fear and was awash with sweat despite the cold weather.

"Who's there?" Anna called out. "Who's there!!." She called again, searching for where she kept her phone. "I'm calling the police." She threatened.

"He´s making a list, he´s checking it twice. He´s gonna find out who is naughty or nice. Santa Claus is coming to town." The voice continued to sing harshly from beneath the bed.

Anna realized it was coming from beneath her and screamed and jumped to her feet on the bed. "Please, who are you?" she cried.

"He sees you when you´re sleeping." He continued without answering her.

"Please," Anna begged him as the tears flowed freely from her eyes. She was sweaty due to fear but the goosebumps on her body gave her chills as well.

"And he knows when you´re awake." He sang strongly.

"Please," Anna begged desperately. She eyed the door, contemplating if she would make it if she made a desperate run.

"He knows if you´ve been bad or good." He sang on, adding extra emphasis on the "bad". "So be good for goodness sake." He spat.

There was a way he sang the last verse that filled Anna with dread and she made her desperate run.

Something collided with her legs from underneath the bed and she tumbled to the floor.

The man crawled out from under the bed and Anna let out a shriek as she saw him.

He was tall and slender. He wore rugged black boots and jeans. He wore a black t-shirt under a black windbreaker.

The most frightening thing about him was his face. It was concealed behind a porcelain mask made to look like Santa Claus.

It had a white face and red rosy cheeks with a large porcelain beard that had been painted white.

"Santa Claus is here." He said to Anna. "He knows if you've been naughty or nice… and you've been a bad girl, Anna." He said. "I saw what you did last week."

Anna's eyes widened and she inched backward for a few meters before getting to her feet and running out of the room.

He ran after her and down the stairs. The sound of his heavy boot each time they landed on the wooden stairs made Anna's heart inch closer to her mouth.

She reached the door and threw it open, happy to have made it.

Rough hands suddenly grabbed her hair and pulled her back into the house as she let out bloodcurdling screams.

The man in the Santa mask threw her into the living room where Anna saw his red sack.

"Help me," Anna screamed at the top of her lungs.

The man gave her a hard backhanded slap across her face and she fell to the floor, zapped of energy.

He picked up a hammer from his sack and two huge iron nails used in construction sights.

He picked her up and held her against the brick wall they hand above the heater to make it look like a chimney.

She pleaded with him gently then let out a long and agonizing scream as the man drove one of the nails through her shoulder and into the wall.

He did the same with the other shoulder till she looked like a morbid stocking hanging over the fireplace. The blood from her wounds seemed into her white nightgown and gradually turned red. Making her look even more like a stocking.

The man went into his sack and produced a few lumps of coal. He forced her mouth open and shoved them in.

"So be good for goodness sake." He sang darkly as he produced a sharp thing knife fashioned like a stick of peppermint candy.

He looked deep into her pleading eyes and in one swift motion slit open her throat.

Anna gurgled and gasped as the blood gushed out of her neck and splattered on the floor.

Her head fell limply forward as she stopped struggling.

"So be good for goodness sake." He said softly and kissed her forehead as he left with the door wide open.

He still had plenty of names to cross off his naughty list.

CHAPTER 2

THE LADY WHO APPEARS DURING CHRISTMAS

My best friend Renold and I lived in the same block. It was the time of Christmas so we were walking around looking at the Christmas trees outside everyone's house. In the midst of darting around, we didn't even realize that we had come a bit too far.

The surrounding was still sunny while we left the house. But moments later we both realized how dark and ominous the environment had got. At that moment, we were closer to the woods than we were to our house.

As we were already near the woods I suggested that we explore. After all, it was Christmas night and our parents would be busy with all the preparations. So, Renold and I began to move farther into the forest. We both were delighted, I raised my face up in the sky, allowing the light from the moon to dance across my skin. Tiny insects hummed in and out of the trees. I was enjoying every moment of it.

Suddenly, there was a peculiar sound. We paused for a while to listen, then Renold assured me that it was the sound of trees lashing against one another. But when I turned behind, I saw a shadow that somewhat resembled a lady.

I didn't mention it to Renold, because I didn't want to freak him out plus I also thought that it could be my imagination.

All of a sudden, I stumbled upon something. I leaned down. It was an old key that had the number "13" engraved. In a split second, Renold yelled, "Look there's a cabin over there!" Excitedly, we ran towards the cabin.

It was old and rusty. I inserted the key and the door opened. As we walked inside the cabin, its door shut itself loudly. Shivers ran down my spine. I trembled inside in terror. In no time, Renold screamed on top of his lungs and stood still shivering. I rushed to find the whole floor covered with blood.

My body became cold. Unexpectedly, I noticed something in the corner of the room. The object captivated my attention. But slowly it began to come towards us and what we saw shook us to our core for the rest of our lives. It was a lady dressed in a white gown. Her hair was all over her dark hollow eyes, blood was dripping down her lips and she had no nose.

I held Renold's hands tightly and began to run away from the cabin. However, the lady walked faster than us and in no time, she came really close to our face. Her smile didn't seem normal, it looked wicked. All at once, she grabbed Renold in an attempt to strangle him, but he dodged and her sharp nails seemed to cut through his skin. The blood oozed out, and the lady began laughing hysterically.

While her attention was on Renold, I kept trying to unlock the front door to escape. Luckily it opened and I pulled Renold along with me. But she whispered "I will come back" then the door shut loudly by itself.

After that, we ran to our homes and kept that incident a secret. Until one day I came across an anonymous storytelling page where a person had written about the same old lady in the same forest on Christmas.

CHAPTER 3

THE VISITOR

A few years ago, I lived in a small town where almost everyone was friendly with one another. It was the proverbial countryside hamlet where there were lush trees and farmlands as far as the eye can see. I worked as a volunteer caregiver for the elderly and it was my job to go to lots of homes where elderly people lived and help around in their daily needs and errands. I love every single one of my charges.

Everyone that is, except for a cantankerous old woman named Mrs. McCree, who lived in the middle of nowhere; which was basically 3 kilometers outside of town. She was civil and polite when necessary, but generally, she was mean and can be quite…unpleasant, for lack of a gentler tone. She would scowl and spit at people who came by; she would even throw some stones at travelers and was especially mean to volunteers and caregivers. I personally didn't like Mrs.

McCree, but as a caregiver, it was my job to make her comfortable regardless of her attitude.

It was during the Christmas holidays and Mrs. McCree was being exceptionally grouchy and mean that almost everyone wanted to avoid talking to her. I sighed as I finished decorating her Christmas tree and prepared her coffee. "Would you like some holiday muffins with your coffee, Mrs. McCree?" I asked.

"Why the hell are you asking if I wanted some saw mill cupcake?" She would reply. "Coffee will be fine, thank you very much." She added in her usual condescending tone.

I kept telling myself that she was just an old woman who had no one else in this world. As the water was heating, there came a knock on the front door. "Get the door!" She barked. I got up and walked to the front door and opened it. A young man stood outside the porch. He wore a thick black coat and had very handsome facial features. I looked to see if he had driven here or something. But I couldn't see any other car other than my own. "Good afternoon." He greeted with a polite tone. "I'm looking for Mrs. Agatha McCree."

"I'm her caregiver. " I replied. "Is there something you need from her?"

"Let's say, I have been meaning to visit her for some time." The young man replied. "May I come in?"

I was very much apprehensive about letting him in. After all, this was the middle of nowhere and the idea of house intruders and robbers was enough to frighten Mrs. McCree to death. Before I could say anything, Mrs. McCree came shuffling towards the door. "Who's that outside? Why are you letting the snow in? Can't you see how cold the house is becoming!? What are you doing standing-"

She stopped midsentence as she reached the door and stared at the young man. "Could it be?" She said softly. " Is it really?"

"I'm here to see you…." The man said. "…Mama."

Mama? So the young man was her son? I had no idea she had relatives nearby. As far as I know, most of her children were either in different states or had passed on. Mrs. McCree then said. "What are you doing just standing there?! Let my son in!"

I quickly gathered myself and invited the young man in. As he walked inside, I offered to take his coat and when his hands touched mine, they were eerily cold. Not the kind of cold you would get when you're out in the cold. It was almost…..a dead kind of cold. I tried to brush it off and watched as grumpy and grouchy Mrs. McCree started to smile and lead 'her son' into the parlor. She instructed me to prepare some hot chocolate for her son. I walked to the kitchen and began preparing some refreshments. I would glance every now and then at the living room where she and the young man were having what looked like a very spirited and lively talk.

Perhaps deep down, she was just lonely and missed her kids. I poured the hot drink from the kettle and as I held it up, I saw something odd being reflected in the kettle's surface. The reflection showed the living room where Mrs. McCree and her son were sitting. Only, her son's reflection wasn't being reflected.

Instead, a dark shadowy mass was shown sitting next to Mrs. McCree. I rubbed my eyes wondering if I was seeing things. I brushed it off once more and took the hot drinks to the living room. I set them down and suddenly felt this heavy uneasiness around me. I couldn't explain it. But one thing was certain, this man made me uneasy and I worried for Mrs. McCree. I then tried to tell Mrs. McCree that it was time for her nap, but she dismissed me, saying that she would be spending her afternoon talking to her son and that I could leave early.

"But, I-" I started.

"That would be all. Take the rest of the day off." Mrs. McCree said. I couldn't argue with her and regardless, if my charges tell me that I was not needed, then I had to obey. I bade her goodbye and told her that I was going to be back the next day. I gathered my things and walked out of the house. I got in my car and began to drive through the snow when I got a call from the head caregiver.

"Oh, you're off early?" He said over the phone. "Mrs. McCree being too much to handle?"

"Today, she's a bit calmer. " I replied. "Her son came to visit her and she looks quite happy."

"Son?" The head caregiver repeated.

"Yeah." I replied. "It looks like it's been awhile since they last spoke. Although I didn't know she had a son."

"Oh she does." The head caregiver replied. "But, the thing is-"What he said next sent chills down my spine. "The thing is, her son's been missing for nearly 25 years. And it was only recently that they found his dead body in an empty lot a few kilometers away. That's why I was calling you to see if you can break the news…"

"Wait!" I said. "If her son's been dead for that long, then who's with Mrs. McCree right now?!" I asked in a panic as I turned the car around and drove back to Mrs. McCree's house. I got out and ran to the front door to see that it was opened. I got in and what I saw next sent even more chills to my spine.

Mrs. McCree was on the floor completely still and hovering above her was the strange shadowy shade that I saw being reflected in the son's place. I saw it suddenly turn its faceless head towards me and before I knew it , I could hear a strange wail before it faded away. I ran towards Mrs. McCree and felt for a pulse. Nothing. She was gone. I couldn't believe what just happened. Or rather, I couldn't explain how it even happened.

When the ambulance came, they asked me what had caused her death. I couldn't simply say that her son came over. It would be very uncanny and odd. Her death was then reported as natural causes. As the ambulance drove away, I began to walk back to my car and as soon as I got inside, I looked at the front door's reflection via my rear view mirror. I can never forget what I saw as I began to drive through the snow.

Standing by the front door was the strange shadowy shade just looking at me with its featureless face.

To this day, Mrs. McCree's house is in ruins. And every time I drive past the house during the holidays, I can still see the shadow

shade just standing there….waiting……waiting…….

CHAPTER 4

Samantha Curley was what the younger generation would term a "celebrity". She had not been featured in any movies or done anything noteworthy, but she has been termed a celebrity due to the high number of followers and friends she had online.

She had a large following on Instagram and was therefore dubbed an "Influencer" She posted a wide variety of videos, ranging from make-up tutorials, fashion-related life hacks, skincare routines, fine dining, and the like. She had a lot of people dedicated to her page, and they followed her posts like social zombies.

At the end of the year, she decided to "give back" to her fans and planned on hosting a Christmas dinner party for a few lucky fans who were also up-and-coming Social Media Influencers at her family's private estate.

To make it fun for everyone and to prevent just anyone from coming, she hid the invitations and made it into a scavenger hunt. Those who found the invites would be given directions to the estate only hours before the party to prevent them from disclosing the location.

The day of the Christmas party came, and over 50 guests had been invited to the private party. The location was secluded, but the mansion was huge and magnificent, the entire length and breadth of the roof was covered in yellow-flashing Christmas lights. The estate was lit up by 18th century streetlamps and the magical yellowish glow, coupled with the falling snow in the background and the Christmas lights, made the mansion look like a picture out of a Christmas card.

There was a life-size Santa Claus on a sleigh, complete with reindeer and elves. And even a quirky snowman. The snow made a satisfactory crunching sound beneath their feet and as the guests marveled at the place, their breaths came out as long ghostlike wisps, making it look like they smoked invincible cigars.

The hall was decorated with fake snow and mistletoe. There was a magnificent, immaculate white Christmas tree with singing Christmas lights and a barrage of fake presents beneath it. The decorations really did portray the festive period. There were golden bells and nutcrackers, party poppers and the works.

The hall was huge and in the middle was a set of long dinner tables attached on end to make one long unbroken table. The table was lined with silver cutlery and empty platters, and the smell of cooking wafted from the kitchen.

There were camcorders and cameras everywhere, and the guests were excited that they would most likely feature in Samantha's next video.
Samantha welcomed her guest and the servants shut the gates and entrances of the estate.

"So, before we begin, I would like you all to know that you're all featuring in my next video, and it's live. Samantha said excitedly while her guests applauded and waved at the cameras.

The video was being streamed, but it wasn't on Instagram or any of the more well-known apps. It was streaming straight to the dark web.

 "So in today's video, I'm going to be teaching you all how to commit a DUI." She continued excitedly while her guests were a little bit confused. "I'm sure you're all wondering about the type of DUI I'm talking about... But don't worry, we're not driving drunk." She said with a laugh. "A DUI simply stands for Death Under an Influence." Samantha finished

"What?" a guest asks with a nervous laugh before a crossbow bolt lodges itself in his eye. He doesn't even have time to cry out before he collapses on the table. The blood from his wound seeped into the white tablecloth and began to spread.

The entire hall exploded into chaos as the guests began to run for dear life. The rest of Samantha's inbred family show up. They're eight in number and all carrying weapons ranging from crossbows to antique hunting rifles, swords and knives, pistols, and a morning star. They handed Samantha a sinister-looking knife, and she runs after one of the guests who has yet to flee the hall. She jumps on his back and begins to stab him viciously, splattering blood everywhere till the man becomes unresponsive. She pulls his neck backwards and smiles at the camera before she slits his throat with the knife. She pushes him away and goes outside.

Her family runs after the others, slaughtering everyone they came across. There are also cameras scattered everywhere to record the slaughter. There were jammers to prevent the guest from calling for help. They all swarmed to the gates, but they were locked, and the walls were too high to climb. Cutting off all escape whatsoever.

The estate was filled with screaming men and women. Some screaming in pain and others in fear. There was the "*oof*" that escaped their lips when they were struck down by bullets or a morning star. There were men and women crawling on the floor, screaming in agony as they had limbs sliced off. There was a particular woman whose arm was only hanging on to her body by a single thread of flesh.

Samantha ran through her guests, slashing and stabbing those she came in contact with. Slitting throats and gouging eyes with a smile, till she was drenched in blood. Each time she was in front of a camera she would lick the blood of her blade and flash her bloody pearly whites.

A few of the guests tried scaling the walls and a servant brought Samantha a hunting rifle. She would wait till they struggled to reach the top then shoot them back down.

It took an hour and a half for her and her family to find and kill everyone. There were bodies in nearly every room in the house. Bodies that had met their deaths in horrible fashions. The compound was even worse. Severed heads and limbs littered everywhere and there were patches of pink and red snow where the victims had bled out.

After the killing was done, she returned to the camera to address her viewers. As the servants dragged the corpses away, leaving a trail of red on the snow. More snow would be poured on it to hide the blood. The corpses would be stripped of their clothing and belongings and burned, while the bodies would be buried a little way from the house with the previous episodes. There was a reason why the vegetation around there was so lush and green.

"Thank you all for tuning in today. Thank you for the massive turnout. We hope you enjoyed today's episode. She said, wiping the blood off her forehead. "Tune in again by midnight on New Year's Eve for our next episode. "Merry Christmas and a Happy New Year."

CHAPTER 5

THE NAUGHTY LIST

This holiday season, I promised myself not to get worked up with shopping, decorating, or cooking! I work myself up every year for one day, yet I still am unfulfilled when it's all over and done. I guess I do it for my family. I have to put up certain appearances, and it's hard being the first-born child of an influential family. Yes, my family is our town's most successful, important, and loved family. We are always under the microscope, and even with all of our popularity, we manage to hide our biggest secret, a secret of greed, murder, and pain.

I crossed off name after name on my Christmas list when my brother barged in. "Hey, big sister, who made your list this year? Who has been naughty?" His hand reached out to grab one curl hanging from my bun.

"I haven't really committed to anyone yet. Every year, this just gets harder and harder." I sat up, looking at his light brown eyes piercing through me.

"Gail, every year you complain. It's honestly not that hard! Think of an asshole who cut you off in traffic or gave you the finger."

"Dashawn, I don't think that's a reason to add them to the naughty list." He stood up with a smirk on his face. "Maybe not, but it's still fun to think about it." I laughed, yet I was not amused.

My father was blasting "Let It Snow" by the infamous Boyz II Men when I heard him yell out for me. I instantly got up to see what he wanted. "Yes, daddy." In front of him were three huge gifts. "Baby, be a doll and help me hide these from your mother. This year, I really outdid myself. It really was so hard to choose which I wanted to surprise her with." I reluctantly nodded while keeping a plastered smile on my face. I tried to do it as fast as possible to avoid seeing my other family members. When I was done, I grabbed my coat, kissed my father, and headed to the door when my mother stormed in with a huge trash bag with a light pink fluid leaking. "Gail, get into your absolute best. Your aunt is on her way, and we know how judgmental she can be." I threw my head back in anguish and ran up the stairs to prepare for the big night.

There were tons of food and drinks around the table, matched with my family's laughter. My mother, father, sister, brother, two aunts, and uncle were all in attendance. This year, we were missing my grandparents and youngest aunt, her husband, and their three kids, which was a delight for me because, in this case, the less, the merrier.

"Time to open these presents," shouted my brother. He ran to the tree and handed my sister, Shawna, a beautifully wrapped gift. "From me, with lots of love, and I was able to do it all by myself this year." My father nodded in agreement. Shawna smiled mischievously and opened it instantly. My stomach turned in fear of what I'd see or who I'd see next. She gasped in delight. "Oh, Dashawn, I'm very pleased." She turned the gift for all to see, and there it was, two arms with a hot comb clinched in its hands. "It's the stylist that didn't want to give back my deposit." The whole family smiled. I looked over at my mother, who looked so pleased. She turned to my father and said, "Ok, ok, my turn. I got you something you've been dying for, or should I say she was dying to make your Christmas night." My whole family laughed in despair.

I walked over to the alcohol when my mother handed my father his gift. He opened it slowly and then giggled with joy. "It's that goddamn Mrs Jenkins," he replied, grabbing her head out of the box. My head spun. "Mom, Mrs Jenkins is Tasha's grandmother. Tasha is my best friend. How could you?" I cried out.

"Excuse me, young lady," my mother answered with anger. "I am tired of this. Every year gets worse and worse, and I can no longer take it." At that moment, I knew I had made the wrong decision. I could feel the energy in the room shift. "I told you, daddy, she's just not the same," said my sister. Our whole family, now focusing on me, started to walk towards me slowly. My brother picked up a fire poker, and my mother rushed over to me and whispered, "You've been naughty, Gail, and you've become a liability. We all see you walking around here acting better than all of us and pretending to be righteous. You done forgot where you came from, and it's time you be reminded…" I felt a painful blow to my head, then darkness…

What felt like an eternity was actually a whole year, a whole year of being in a vegetable state. Although I was naughty, I didn't make the list, or I wouldn't be here! And every year, my family made it a point for me to be there in silence, watching them exchange the body parts of those who crossed them, constantly reminding me that it could have been my limbs in one of those boxes!

-27-

CHAPTER 6

THE CHRISTMAS I LOST MY FREEDOM

Not every road trip is memorable. For some, you don't want to think back again. Yes, you heard me right. Christmas Eve in 1999 was nothing but horrific and terrifying. I, along with my cousins Alicia, Rody, and Carmen, jumped in my new Ford pickup for a road trip to celebrate the holidays with my family. We had no GPS, so Mapquest was the place to go. But there was only one condition; pay attention to the roads because using Mapquest was known to get people lost. However, after a few hours of driving, we noticed we had lost our way and had been reaching the same spot continuously. We were soon panic-ridden. What was even worse was that soon the grey clouds hovered in the sky, and it began to rain and snow uncontrollably. I had difficulties trying to drive while the rain was pouring down vigorously. On top of that, the visibility was also not that great. So, we all decided to stay inside the vehicle until the rain stopped. During those days, we didn't have mobile phones like today. We were contactless with our other family and friends. But we were still glad that we had one another, which gave us hope to escape from that mysterious jungle. In a bit of time, we all slumbered in the car.

Nevertheless, at around 3 am, I abruptly woke up with my stomach grumbling like crazy and with utmost weakness. I felt darkness overshadow my eyes. Abruptly, a loud, screeching noise caught my attention. It seemed like someone had been crying in agony. I rubbed my eyes and managed to open them. To my surprise, my cousins were no longer in the car. I felt a shiver run down my spine. I was completely terrified. "Guys?" I yelled out upon pulling down my window. When I didn't get any response, I decided to get out of the car and look for them. As I exited my pickup, I felt a cold breeze gently run down my spine again. "Who is it?" I mumbled softly upon abruptly turning behind. There was no one, which made me even more frantic with fear. Dread twisted in my gut. As a response, I instinctively began to look for my cousins. "Alicia! Rody! Carmen!" I yelled their names.

When I didn't get any reply back, I stood there, wide awake in a haze of fear. My heart pounded rapidly. With my cold and clammy hands, I wiped off my sweat while looking around for my cousins. Suddenly, I stumbled upon something. Quite reluctantly, I kneeled to feel it. It could be anything, wild animal or reptile, I believed. But as I glanced, my body shook. I had stumbled upon a human body that still felt warm, dressed in an Elf sweater and dirty jeans. I turned on the flashlight and pin-pointed it on the face. It didn't take me long to distinguish that it was Alicia's body. I screamed in fear and tried to run around nonchalantly, looking for Rody and Carmen, but it seemed fate had other plans for me that night. Soon, I also found their dead bodies aligned in a long line. Extremely startled, I began to put the corpses in the back seat of my pickup because there was no way I could leave them there.

As I did that, I noticed someone staring at me from a distance. Before I could even discern, it came really close to my face wearing a filthy ripped Santa sweater. Its eyes were pushed deep into their sockets. There were two holes in place of the nose, and it had no mouth. I gulped and became extremely nervous. Not a single word managed to escape from my mouth. However, the strange entity in front of my face began to laugh hysterically. Its laughter echoed inside the jungle as I stood there with my legs shivering. "It's your turn now!" It yelled and tried to lunge at me. I was confused and deeply terrified all at the same time. So, I pushed the entity and hopped inside my car. I managed to get inside the car safely, but the entity kept trying to open the doors. Finally, I was able to accelerate the car and move forward. I checked the time; it was past 4 am. Abruptly, I felt something crash on top of my car. My heart slammed against my ribs in fear as I inhaled the cold air from the AC to slow down my breathing. I kept trying to convince myself that it was my imagination. But deep down, I knew it wasn't because it soon came down to my front windshield. I comprehended that it was no other than the horrifying being I had seen earlier. I began to drive my vehicle at full speed. Finally, the entity vanished into thin air. I took a breath of relief, but it didn't last long. In a bit of time, I noticed it walking towards my car from my rearview mirror. In a bid to make an escape, I drove at full speed, not knowing where I was headed. I don't know if it was my lucky day or unlucky day. I managed to reach the town. Nevertheless, the police had been tracking my fast-moving truck for some time. They stopped me and demanded a check inside. I tried to tell them the truth, but no one believed me because they found the dead bodies of my cousins inside the trunk of my pickup.

Since then and every Christmas going forward, I have been living in the high-security mental asylum, where no one believes that I'm innocent. I relive that moment every day, and during Christmas, I often get a visit from the entity with the filthy Christmas sweater and sucked-in eyes.

-32-

CHAPTER 7

THE CHRISTMAS GIFT

I was studying at a university in Calgary, nearly five thousand miles from home. My days were mostly dull and boring. However, that night before Christmas, I received a postcard from my parents. "Merry Christmas our little munchkin, we have bought an apartment for you!"

As soon as I read the message. I jumped as high as the ceiling. Honestly, I was overjoyed since I was fed up with staying in a shared room dorm.

I thanked my parents and moved into the new apartment the very next day. Best Christmas gift of all time! I said to myself as I unlocked the door to my very first apartment.

The fresh paint lingered around the one-bedroom apartment. The space was huge. It was fully furnished.

Nevertheless, the apartment itself was still under construction and not many people had moved it. Probably that is the reason why it was a lot cheaper.

Above my room was the top floor that had a suite still under construction.

One by one I brought all the stuff to my room beside the study table. So, I think around 10 pm I went downstairs and brought my study table. As I was walking towards my room I noticed a strange figure at the end of the hallway.

Even though it was quite dark, I could sense that the odd figure was glaring at me. Suddenly, my eyes landed upon its peculiar feet that almost looked crooked.

Slowly, it crept towards me. The nearer it came, the more discrete its face looked. He made direct eye contact with me and began coming closer.

It had broad white ghoulish eyes, pale burnt skin, two holes in the place of the nose, and an uncanny frown. I never used to get scared easily, but his face made the shivers run down my spine. I was terrified and began running towards my flat.

As I reached my flat, I tried to calm myself down thinking it was just my imagination. However, that night I had an unusual dream. The kind of dream that still haunts me to this day.

I saw the same guy unlocking my door and entering my bedroom. Before I could even say anything. The guy came close to my face and began to cut his mouth. Blood dripped down his face as he stood there laughing like a maniac.

Slowly, his eyes turned white and ghoulish and suddenly he began to chase me around. In order to keep me safe. I ran towards the living room and hid underneath the table. My body was trembling in fear. Abruptly, my bedroom door opened and I could see a dark shadow looming inside. Before I managed to run away, the guy found me. He kneeled down at the table and stared at me with a grin on his face.

I tried to run but the guy grabbed my hand tightly and pulled me out. I could feel nothing but blind terror, but somehow managed to push the guy and stab him. The guy screamed in agony. His screech echoed inside the empty room and blood splattered all over the white freshly painted walls in the living room.

Then, I woke up covered in sweat. What a nightmare! I thought to myself as I began the take a deep breath of relief. I got up to grab a glass of water, but I saw a strange blue bruise on my hand and blood on both of my hands. Shivers ran down my spine. I was confused. Then, I rushed to the living room to find the walls covered in blood and a guy lying on the floor.

I ran downstairs in fear to call the guard, but when he came up. There was nothing. Not even a hint of blood. I was terrified. And left that apartment that instant. To this day I have never returned back to that place and I've also heard that the owners of the apartment went bankrupt and the building remains abandoned.

CHAPTER 8
KURT & OLIVIA

"Merry Christmas," I heard my boyfriend yell out from the dining room. I was still half asleep when I grabbed my phone to check the time. "Kurt, it's 6 AM. Are you trying to wake up the whole building?"

"Maybe. It's Christmas morning, darling. I hardly think anybody in this building is still asleep! Especially those with children," he chuckled.

I'd been dating Kurt for some time now, four years to be exact, and I truly felt I'd met my soulmate. He was tall, dark, and handsome, with gorgeous hazel eyes. He was the life of the party, his confidence was unbelievable, and he could talk to anyone. I envied him for these. His family migrated to the states from Haiti when he was just two. He spoke four languages, graduated top of his class, and was an electrical engineer. He was perfect! Then you have me; I was 5'1, overweight, and with curly frizzy hair. I was a high school dropout that lucked out with a really good career at her mother's law firm. I had always been the disappointment of the family. While my sisters and brothers had great careers, such as doctors and big-time executives, I chose to opt out of school pretty early. I was regular as they came and, might I add, not talkative. I'd always been a bit shy. Kurt was literally my better half, and I did just about anything to keep him.

 "I'm not excited about today. You know how I feel being around my family for too long," I sighed. I watched Kurt hide something in his dingy old bag. "Did you hear me, or are you too busy trying to hide something from me?" His eyes were peeled at me. Man is he beautiful, I thought to myself.

"OK, OK, you got me. It's your Christmas gift. I wanted to give it to you later unless you would like to open it now." I smiled with delight and held my hand out with my eyes sealed tightly when I felt a paper hit my hand.

"I was expecting a jewelry box, maybe a ring."

"Olivia, this is almost as good as getting a ring," he said while looking at me seductively. The paper was heavy as if it was a contract of some sort. It was two tickets to the Dominican Republic. I jumped up with joy. "A vacation, Curt!"

"Don't get too happy now until you see the second part of the gift." I ruffled through the papers to see "PAID IN FULL" in red. "I give up. What are you trying to show me?" He looked at me with his eyes full of excitement and blurted out, "It's a BBL. I got you a BBL."

I stood there with a confused look on my face and started to feel insecure about myself immediately. I walked over to my closet to avoid him seeing the disappointment on my face. I felt his hand touch my shoulder.

"I paid for you to get a BBL. Remember you told me a month ago that's what you wanted before your birthday."

"I know I said that, but I see a lot of things that I don't mean, and you getting me this shows that you are not happy with how I look."

"What? Are you kidding me right now? I thought I was doing something good for you. I want you to feel every bit of how beautiful I think you are."

My eyes filled with tears. "I hate you because you always know just what to say to make me feel better." he opened up his arms and walked over to me, waiting for a hug.

"So, do you forgive me? I can cancel it and do something else for you."

I cut him off before he could finish his sentence. "I am happy, Kurt, and I want to look my best for you. So yes, I will go through with the BBL." His smile warmed my soul.

"It's beginning to look a lot like Christmas, Olivia."

With my birthday only being three months away and knowing that the healing process takes about the same amount of time, we decided to go three days after Christmas. I wanted to bring the new year in with my new body and, hopefully, with more confidence than I ever had.

"I am worried about you, Olivia, "said my mother as she helped me pack my suitcase. I tried to ignore her, but she just kept going on. "And if Kurt has so much money, why is he booking doctors in other countries? "

"Mom, it has nothing to do with the funds. It's more like the body they give you in those countries is far better than they can do here, and…." I stopped talking because the look on her face said it all. The look of worry made me realize that this was something serious. I walked over and kissed her on the forehead. "Don't worry about me, mom. I'll be OK." Will I be OK? I thought in my head.

The day of the trip came rather quickly, and I was a total wreck! I had barely slept the night before and kept thinking over and over about what it was that I was about to do. "Kurt, are you sure you looked into this doctor?" I was twirling my hair in my fingers, not trying to hide my anxiety. The look he gave me reassured me that I would be fine and before he could even say anything, I held my hand out to his. "What am I saying? I trust you." He grabbed my hand, looked at me, and said, "Good."

The airplane ride was not as bad as I expected. We sat in first class, and I was excited to have that privilege! The whole plane ride, I went on so many shopping sites, such as Fashion Nova, PLT, and my favorite, Skims. I envisioned my body and what it would look like. I would finally look like the girls on Instagram! My waist would be small, and my breasts would be nice, large, and round with the perfect bubble butt to match. I thought of myself in so many dresses and crop tops that I never had the confidence to wear. I started to realize this might be a good thing. Maybe this will be what I need to get the confidence I feel I deserve.

I woke up to loud cheers and claps. "Hey, sleepyhead, we arrived."

With a puzzled look on my face, I whispered, "Why is everybody clapping and cheering?" Kurt burst out into laughter. "Girl, you Americans know nothing. It's what people do when they arrive in their country of origin. They are happy to be home." I giggled and started to take in the ambiance around me. I hugged Kurt and thanked him again. I truly was lucky to have him.

As we walked through the airport hand in hand, I felt a bit of relief seeing more American girls who were probably here for the same reason as me. They were in groups, talking loudly. The bonnets and pajamas showed they wanted to fly in comfort. I stared up until I saw a short girl with long braids who caught my attention. She rolled her eyes at me, then placed her eyes on Kurt. She stared with passion in her eyes. I smiled and put my head up, knowing he was all mine. Then, I noticed so many beautiful women with beautiful brown complexions with long jet-black hair that were freshly done. And let me not get started on their bodies! I was in amazement at just how perfect it looked. I could see Kurt trying not to look, so I nudged him. "It's OK. I'm looking too." We both laughed, squeezing each other's hands.

Sudden humidity hit my face when I exited the airport. My back started to sweat immediately, and I had a big sweater on. I looked over at Kurt, who had sweat forming on his head. "It sure is hot out here. If I knew, I would've worn something more revealing."

"Me too." We giggled while staring at each other like two children with a crush. Our giggles came to a stop when a short man with sunglasses approached us. He had on a yellow Polo shirt with khaki green shorts that looked a bit dingy. His hair was dark as night, and his skin was pale with acne on his cheeks. He had braces and spoke very fast in Spanish. Kurt responded in Spanish; he spoke so beautifully, and I was impressed with him all over again. Kurt went into his pocket and handed the man twenty dollars. "What was that for? "I stepped back to get a clear look at his face. "Olivia, a lot of these people in this country are poor. He asked if I could help him get diapers for his baby, and I couldn't deny a man trying to do right by his family." I smiled ear to ear and thought to myself how really lucky I was to have him.

A gold Toyota pulled up. The driver grabbed our bags and started loading them in his trunk. He spoke Spanish even faster than the last guy, but Kurt could still respond. We hopped into the car, excited for our journey to the hotel. There were so many young kids on the sides of the road on dirt bikes. I was pretty sure the women were selling themselves based on the way they were dressed. Cars blasted Spanish music, and stray cats and dogs roamed the street looking for scraps to eat. I was taken aback by how poor the country actually looked. At that moment, I felt bad for the people of the Dominican Republic until I noticed how happy some of them were. I watched in amazement, wondering what it would be like to live here.

After 45 minutes in the city, the area started to look more rural and country-like. I turned over to Kurt, who was sleeping with his mouth open. "Babe, How far is this place?" With his hand in his pocket, he reached for his phone.

"I was told the hotel was only 15 minutes from the airport. I dozed off, expecting the Uber driver to know where we were going. I'm sorry." Before I could say anything, he started to talk to the driver in Spanish. With every exchange of words, I could hear the aggression in both voices. I tried to chime in.

"Excuse me, sir."

He instantly turned around with his eyes off the road. "Cállate la puta chica blanca."

I had no clue what he said, but he made my heart skip a beat. Kurt sat up with anger, and I felt the car jerk and pull off to the side of the road. The car came to a complete stop, and the driver jumped out of the car, opened my door, and pulled me out. Before I could scream, I glanced at about four or five men coming from the bushes. I watched in horror as they grabbed Kurt and hit him with a 2 x 4. Suddenly, I felt a pain in my head, and there was darkness.

 I awakened to cries and sharp pain on the side of my skull. I tried to sit up when I heard, "The princess is up." I looked around and saw several people tied up, tears covering their faces while trying to remain quiet. We were surrounded by trees. The man motioned me to stand up, yet all I could do was look around for Kurt.

"Where is …"

The man replied, "Your privilege does not exist here. Give me all of your jewelry." I started to take it off, still moving my head around, searching for Kurt. I recognized a familiar face. It was the girl from the airport with the long braids, her face full of fear. She looked at me, and for some reason, I felt some comfort, but not for long. The man in front of me pulled out a gun. "Stop looking around and give me everything you have." His English was terrible, and his breath smelled of rum. I started to cry and hold my face. He hit me and grabbed my hair. I screamed.

"I don't have anything else."

Pushing me down to the ground, he walked over to a man holding on to his wife and shot him in the head. My body was consumed with terror. I went limp and cried silently.

Finally, an older gentleman with dark skin and a scar on his forehead approached us. He handed more rope to some of his men, and they tied us up tightly. We walked in a single file and deeper into the wooded area. I was tapped on my back. I looked over to see a young man, no older than 15, with a rifle. He was skinny and tall with chapped lips and a lisp. He asked me in perfect English, "Aren't you looking for him?" I turned around to see what he was pointing at when I dropped to my knees, screaming and crying. I felt pain in my heart, and every beautiful moment we shared started playing in my head. There he was, the love of my life. There he was, tied to a tree, beaten to death. His face was covered in blood, and his jaw was pulled down, barely still attached to his face. His beautiful teeth were mangled, and his left eye was gone. I could not believe my eyes, and I couldn't move a muscle in my body. I screamed and cried with my face in the dirt. The young man clutched my shirt. "He didn't want to listen and comply. He chose his fate," he said.

I stood to my feet and started to walk, but I couldn't take my eyes off the man who made me feel like the luckiest girl alive! And I started to feel guilty. Had I not asked for this BBL and had some form of confidence, I wouldn't be in this position! Kurt would still be here. The thoughts ran through my head. My self-esteem, which I always battled with, had made me lose the best thing that ever happened to me! I'd lost the man that I was going to marry, the future father of my children because I was so self-absorbed and wanted what I felt was today's standards of beauty. I synced into my skin, waiting for the moment of my death! Hell, I didn't care. Without Kurt, I was already dead.

We finally arrived at an area with water, trees, and a small cabin that looked old and rugged. The men placed us near the water with our backs towards them. I heard a loud bang that sounded like a firecracker, but instead, it was the gun. It was my first time ever hearing a gun within earshot. With each bang, I saw blood pour into the water, and a body floated away. I caught a glance at the girl with the long braids and the frightening look she had on her face. We made eye contact. The young man walked over and shot the person next to her. She kept her eyes locked with mine, knowing she would meet her end. As the person next to her floated away in the water, she still stared at me. The young man walked behind her. She closed her eyes, took a deep breath, and sighed. Bang! Her eyes open, she dropped to her knees with her mouth agape. I paused in horror, watching her soul leave her body.

Through every shot, I became more numb. I already felt the fear. I tried bargaining in my head with God. I tried to bargain with God and ask him to give me one more day and the things that I would do if I could just survive this. And then, finally, the acceptance of my death. I now understood why my mother was so worried and the anger I felt that she might never know what happened to me! My brothers, my sisters. I was supposed to be my best friend's maid of honor! Now, look at me. I was going to be the girl that went missing in another country with her boyfriend. His steps were getting closer. Bang! The girl next to me fell into the water. I accepted my death. I was loved, and Kurt made me feel like the luckiest girl alive. The young man walked behind me. I heard the gun cock. Bye-bye, princess. I heard a bang and blood splatter. I felt myself collapse, my mind felt paralyzed, and my body was stripped of its ability to remain conscious. I comprehended what was happening, and then darkness befell.

CHAPTER 9

THE HOLIDAY HITCHHIKER

When we were a lot younger, our mom taught us to always do an act of random kindness. It could come in the form of simply paying for someone's meal or helping someone cross the street or even giving rides to total strangers and hitchhikers. My best friend and I would go on many road trips and midnight drives and on occasion, we would encounter hitchhikers needing a ride and we would often give them one. Especially if there was no bus in sight and the weather was not favorable.

It was the Christmas holidays and my best friend and I were hired to play Santa's helpers at a Mall Santa event. We set up the Santa seat, putting up the gift props and even decorating the tree. Once the event started, my best friend and I would guide the kids who lined up to see Santa. It was a really fun and engaging event and just seeing the kids' faces light up whenever they would ask Santa for something was like watching my 8 year old self.

When the event was done, the organizer paid us our fee and thanked us. "Thanks so much for coming." He said. "I know it was such short notice and you probably had to adjust your schedules or something"

"It's no trouble at all." I said. "We're just glad to help."

The organizer thanked us once more, then we made our way to the parking lot, got into the car and began our long drive home. We drove down the dimly lit road, taking care to drive extra carefully since it had been snowing as of late and the roads were quite slippery.

We drove a few more miles along the road when we saw someone standing at the edge of the road sticking their thumb out. What was a person doing out in the snow? I thought. I looked at my best friend, who had the same look as I did. We both nodded and I drove to the side of the road and lowered my window to speak to the person.

I saw the person was a woman and she was dressed in a long red dress and an apron. She had a bonnet on her head, the kind you would see in kid illustrations of a sweet grandma. I looked at the woman. She was a bit older than us with pale blonde hair that had wisps of gray and white strands, a slightly gaunt face that looked as if she hadn't eaten much and eyes looked like she was lost.

"Do you need a ride?" I asked through the window.

The woman looked at me and my friend and nodded. "Yes. I haven't been able to get a ride."

Not in this kind of weather and place, I thought to myself as I invited her into the car. She got into the backseat and sat herself down and closed the door. I started the car engine and began to drive once more. I looked at the woman via the rear view mirror. She just sat there silently, but her face looked like she was brooding; as if she was contemplating on doing something.

"So, where are you headed?" My best friend asked the woman. The woman was silent. She then asked what she was doing in the middle of nowhere. Again, the woman was silent.

I have picked up a lot of hitchhikers before and more often than not, these hitchhikers are the talkative type. They will tell you their life story and where they're headed and would just make drive even more comfortable and nice. This woman, however, was different. I don't know how to explain it, but I was getting extremely uncomfortable with her. Especially when she would just be silent or would just stare at us from time to time.

Still, I offered to help her. "You know, you could tell us where you're headed so that we can drive you there." I said.

The woman looked at me via the rear view mirror and then spoke. "I'm going…..home."

"Okay, where's that?" I asked. I didn't realize then, but we were driving further into a dimly lit road. The woman then began to grin and let out a terrifying cackle that seemed to come from the depths of hell itself. She then lifted her head and we saw a completely different woman.

Her blonde hair was now stringy and white that seemed to jot out from every portion of her head. Her gaunt face had been stretched across her now skeletal face and her sullen eyes were wide and yellow with malice. Her hands were now withered and claw-like. She then got up from her seat and suddenly reached out from behind and grabbed the steering wheel. To our horror, she started to take control of the steering wheel and began to drive quite erratically.

The roads were dark and I couldn't see if there was a pothole or a tree or anything. All I could think of was that this strange woman was trying to crash the car with all of us in it. I tried to regain control of the steering wheel, but the woman was unusually strong and didn't want to let go. I could see my best friend was terrified and was tugging at the woman to let go. But the woman was firm with her grip and was making the car swerve left and right. Our hearts jumped out of our chests when we saw two bright lights coming towards us. It was a truck and this strange cackling woman dressed like a demented Mrs. Clause was careening the car towards the truck. We were going to crash into it if we didn't do anything.

My best friend and I looked at each other. There was nothing we could do except unbuckle our seatbelts, opened our doors and taking a deep breath, we quickly jumped out of our car and rolled into the street. We heard the car crash so we looked up to see. To our surprise, the car stood still and was completely unscathed. The truck had stopped and was just a few inches away from the car. We heard the crash, but the vehicles were alright. I then walked to my car and looked at the backseat.

It was empty!

The strange woman was gone. I looked around the road for any footprints or evidence that she got out, but there was nothing. The driver who had been driving the truck was walking towards us and asked us if we were alright. "Yes, we are." I replied. "Did you see a woman just now?"

"What woman?" He asked. "I didn't see anyone."

"We picked up this woman." My best friend started describing the woman. "She started acting strange and then she grabbed the wheel and was trying to crash the car."

"I haven't seen any woman." The driver said. "But, let me call an ambulance for you and a tow truck for your car. It's not safe driving in these parts. Most people might go nuts and see things that aren't there."

We were still confused as to what just happened, but we accepted the man's offer to help and a few minutes later, the car was being towed and we were in an ambulance getting treated. While we were being tended to, I looked through the ambulance door window and saw the woman dressed in the Mrs. Claus garb standing by the edge of the road just staring back at us and giving us that same eerie smile. I blinked once more and when I looked, she was gone.

To this day, I don't know exactly who the woman was or why it happened or what her intentions were. But one thing's for certain, I'm very much guarded when it comes to picking up hitchhikers during the holidays. Because every time I do pick up a hitchhiker, what I usually see being reflected in my rear view mirror is that strange woman sitting in the back seat, just brooding and giving off that same malicious smile.

CHAPTER 10
DIRTY SANTA

His eyes were bloodshot red. I looked down at his suit, which was covered in dirt. I stared at a beard that was supposed to be white, yet it was dingy and unkempt. I watched each child plop down on this man's lap, yelling out their Christmas requests. He seemed a bit annoyed as he let out a fake smile. As I got closer, I couldn't help but grip my niece's hand tighter. I kneeled down and whispered, "Camilla, if you aren't comfortable talking to Santa, then you don't have to."

"I'm not scared of Santa. I'll kick him like this…." She made a turn motion while waving her two little legs in the air. I chuckled a bit, still holding her close to me. After standing in line for 20 minutes, it was finally her turn. Camilla finally got a good look at him and yelled, "I don't want to go up there. He's an ugly Santa."

He whipped his head around and barked loudly. "Little girl, that's not kind. You insulted Santa a day before Christmas."

"I'm sorry, Santa, she just turned 4. She doesn't know any better," I immediately apologized. He stood up and rushed over to us as if he was going to sock me.

"Well, maybe you should teach her how to respect her elders." The smell of booze followed right behind him.

I couldn't hold back. I covered my nose and responded in a low voice, "Are you drunk, sir? You stink." Everyone around us laughed loudly.

He stepped back. "Did you just embarrass Santa?"

I tried to walk away when I felt a jerk on my shoulder. "Don't fuckin touch me, you hear me? Don't you ever fuckin touch me." He stared me in the eye, and I didn't blink.

"You'll regret this. Oh, you will." He walked off while slowly limping.

The drive home was pretty quiet.

"Titi, do you think the dirty Santa is going to find and kill us? He probably has a knife," I heard my niece ask.

"Camilla, god no, why would you say that?"

She kept staring out the window and let out a sigh. "I'm just scared, Titi. I'm scared he's going to get us."

I remained quiet. I didn't want to ask her anything else because it was no point in getting her all worked up. We finally arrived at my house, and to my surprise, my garage door was opened. I drove up, parked, and tried to close it, but it was jammed. And I was too tired to fuss with it all night. I grabbed my niece and ran into the house as fast as I could.

I couldn't explain why I was so scared all of a sudden. Actually, I was terrified. I sat next to my niece, grabbed my cat, and waited for my husband to return from his work trip. I woke up to a big bang in my garage. I jumped up and checked on my niece. "Jeff, is that you?" I stood by the door, waiting for his reply. When I didn't hear it, my heart started to beat fast!

"Jeff?" Still no reply. I looked over my shoulder to see if my niece was OK. She was still on the couch, sound asleep. My heart was pounding, and sweat started to form on my forehead. I felt my stomach turn. As I turned my doorknob to open my garage door, I felt something push me back. Barging inside, and in a scream, I heard, "I told you that you would regret this."

Before he could come any closer, I kicked him with all my might in his private area and screamed, "Camilla, run, run." My niece popped up and started to scream as this man charged towards me, yet my main focus was to protect her. He grabbed my legs and started dragging me around the house while laughing and striking me every so often. Before he could drag me up the stairs, I reached over, using every bit of my core, and bit him as hard as I could. He screamed and held onto his leg as I ran away to find Camilla. I zoomed into the living room with my eyes full of tears, searching for my niece. I was able to find her by her soft cries. She was behind the couch in a fetal position, clutching her doll. My heart broke, and I knew I had to get her to safety. I carried her into the closet and locked it. We both cried quietly. The footsteps got closer and closer, and then they stopped.

"Titi, do you think he left?"

"Shhhh, I don't know." All I could think about was getting her out of the house. "Camilla, I need you to be a big girl and run to the neighbors house no matter what! Even if Titi falls, just run, OK? Can you do that for me?" Her eyes were covered in tears, and with a little pout on her face, she nodded her head slowly. Now it was time for our escape. I gathered my thoughts and started to push the door open with caution. I looked to my left and slowly to my right. Nothing in sight, I reached out, and Camilla clutched my hand. I placed my finger over my mouth to be sure she remained quiet. We ran fast through the hall and dining room, and finally, I spotted the door. I ran and turned the knob when I felt a sharp pain in my back. I turned to look at my niece as I fought to breathe. I was able to scream, "Run."

Turning to me, she sprinted with a look of terror in her eyes. I felt myself lift off the ground. As I was being picked up, I heard, "I told you you're going to regret this. I kept my promise." My body went limp, and as my last thought entered my head, I thought, "He sure did keep his word."